To Byron

Dial Books for Young Readers • Penguin Young Readers Group
An imprint of Penguin Random House LLC • 375 Hudson Street, New York, NY 10014

Copyright © 2017 by Jon Agee

Printed in China • 9780399538520 • 10 9 8 7 6 5 4 3 2 1

Design by Lily Malcom • Text set in Sentinel

LIFE ON MARS

JON AGEE

Dial Books for Young Readers

I am on Mars.

I have traveled a long way from Earth.

I am here to find life.

Everybody thinks I'm crazy.
Nobody believes there is life on Mars.
But I do. And I just know that I'm going
to find it.

So far, Mars looks pretty gloomy. More gloomy than
I thought. I'm starting to wonder—

could anything possibly live here?

I've brought this gift of chocolate cupcakes.
I don't think I'll find anybody to eat them.

Wow. I was wrong. Mars is nothing but
miles and miles of rocks and dirt!
It's obvious. Nothing could possibly
live here!

What a disaster.

Everybody was right: There is no life on Mars!

I'm going home immediately.

Uh-oh. Where is my spaceship?

I can't believe it.
I'm lost!
Lost on Mars, where
there is no life.

Wait a minute. What's that?

No way! It's life!
It's on Mars, and it's alive!

What an amazing discovery! I can't wait to get
back to Earth and show everybody what I found.

And look—my box of cupcakes! How did it get there?

Now I've got to find my spaceship.
I bet I'll get a good view from the
top of that mountain.

Aha! There it is!

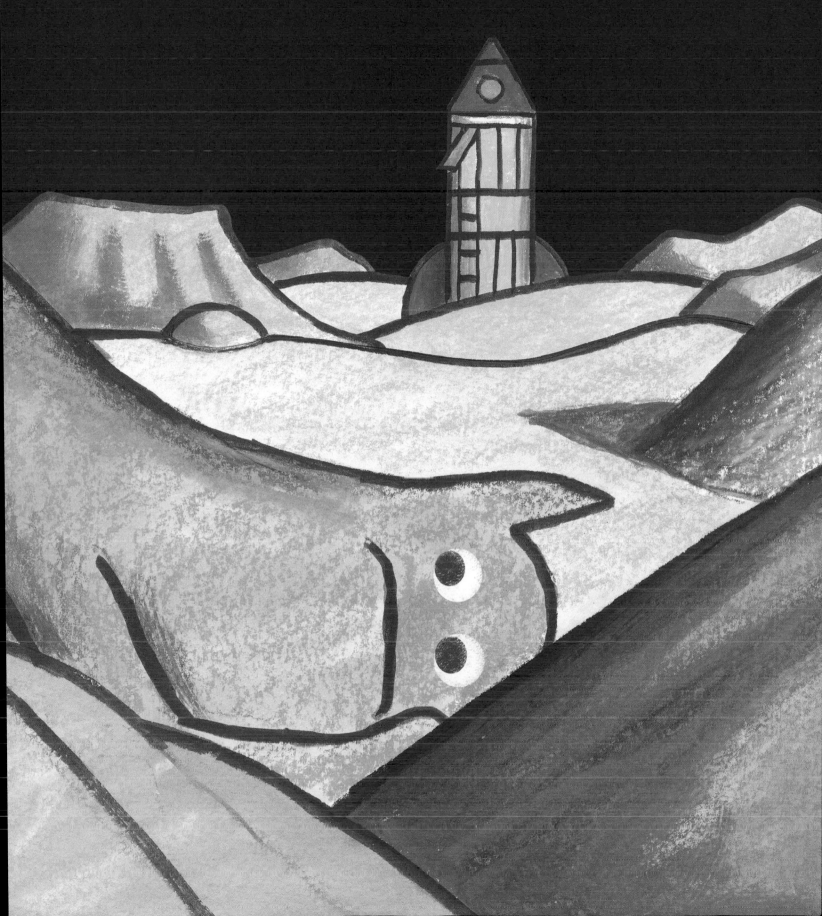

What an adventure!
I always believed there was life on Mars—
and I was right!

I think I deserve a treat.